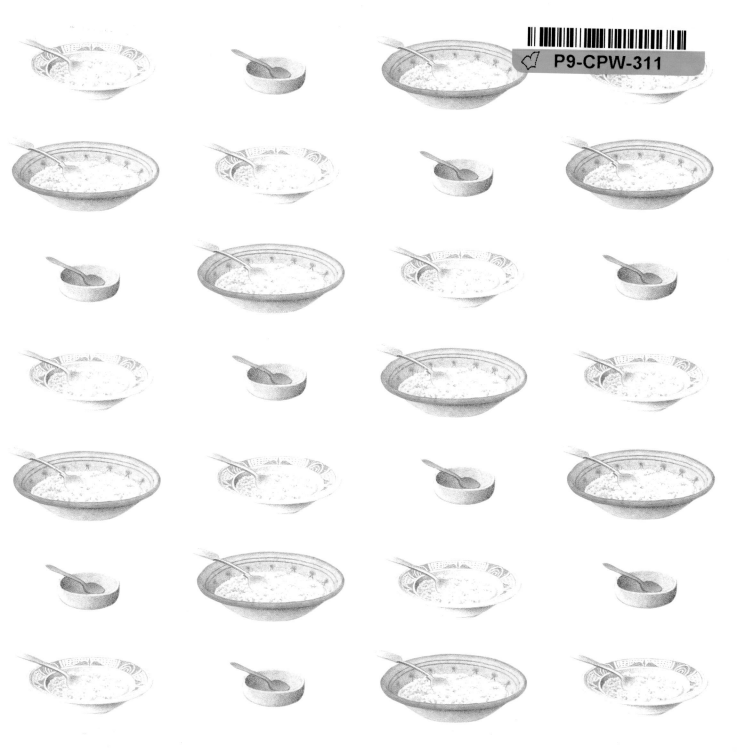

To Terry – NM

Adapted from Robert Southey's original, 1837

First American Edition, 1998

2 4 6 8 10 9 7 5 3 1

DK Publishing, 95 Madison Avenue, New York, New York 10016

Visit us on the World Wide Web at http://www.dk.com

Text copyright © 1998 Dorling Kindersley Ltd.
Illustrations copyright © 1998 Norman Messenger

Library of Congress Cataloging-in-Publication Data

The three bears / adapted from Robert Southey's The story of the three bears :
illustrated by Norman Messenger. – 1st ed.
p.   cm. – (Nursery classics)
Summary: A little girl walking in the woods finds the house of
the three bears and helps herself to their belongings.
ISBN 0-7894-2067-8
[1. Folklore. 2. Bears – Folklore.]   I. Southey, Robert, 1774-1843.
Story of the three bears.   II. Messenger, Norman, ill.
III. Goldilocks and the three bears.   English.   IV. Series.
PZ8.1.T38   1998
398.22–dc21   97–40438
                                                                          CIP
                                                                          AC

Color reproduction by Dot Gradations
Printed and bound by Tien Wah Press, Singapore

The Three Bears

ADAPTED FROM ROBERT SOUTHEY'S
"THE STORY OF THE THREE BEARS"

ILLUSTRATED BY NORMAN MESSENGER

A DK INK BOOK
DK PUBLISHING, INC.

ONCE UPON A TIME

there were Three Bears who lived

together in a house in a wood.

One of them was a
Small, Wee Bear,

one was a
Middle-sized
Bear,

and the
third was a
Great,
Huge Bear.

One day, after the Three Bears had
made porridge for their breakfast,
they walked out into the woods while
the porridge was cooling.

A little girl came to
the house and peeped
in at the keyhole.

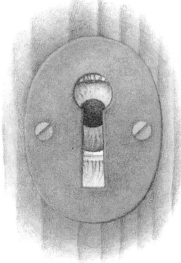

Seeing nobody inside, she lifted the latch and went in. The door was not locked, because the Bears were good Bears, who never suspected that anybody would harm them.

The girl was pleased to see the porridge.
If she had been good, she would have
waited for the Bears to ask her to breakfast.
But she set about helping herself.

First she tasted the
porridge of the
Great, Huge Bear,
and that was too
hot for her.

Then she tasted
the porridge of
the Middle Bear,
and that was
too cold for her.

Then she tasted the
porridge of the Small,
Wee Bear, and
that was just right.
She ate it all up.

Then the girl sat
in the chair of the
Great, Huge Bear,
and that was too
hard for her.

Then she sat in the
chair of the Middle
Bear, and that was
too soft for her.

Then she sat in the chair of the Small,
Wee Bear, and that was just right.
There she sat till the bottom of
the chair came out, and
down came hers,
plump upon
the ground.

Then the girl went upstairs into the bedroom. First she lay upon the bed of the Great, Huge Bear, but that was too high at the head for her.

Next she lay upon
the bed of the
Middle Bear, and
that was too high
at the foot for her.

Then she lay upon the bed of
the Small, Wee Bear, and
that was just right. So she
covered herself up and
fell fast asleep.

By this time the Three Bears thought
their porridge would be cool enough,
so they came home to breakfast.

Now the girl had left the spoon of the
Great, Huge Bear standing in his porridge.

"Someone's been eating my porridge!"

said the Great, Huge Bear, in his great, rough, gruff voice.

And when the Middle Bear looked at his, he saw that the spoon was standing in it, too. **"Someone's been eating my porridge!"** said the Middle Bear, in his middle voice.

Then the Small, Wee Bear looked at his,
but the porridge was all gone.

"Someone's been eating my porridge,
and it's all gone!"

said the Small, Wee Bear,
in his small, wee voice.

The Three Bears began to look around them. Now the girl had left the hard cushion crooked when she rose from the chair of the Great, Huge Bear.

"Someone's been sitting in my chair!"

said the Great, Huge Bear,
in his great, rough, gruff voice.

The girl had squashed down the soft cushion of the Middle Bear.

"Someone's been sitting in my chair!" said the Middle Bear, in his middle voice.

And you know what the girl
had done to the third chair.

"Someone's been sitting in my chair,
and they broke it!"

said the Small, Wee Bear,
in his small, wee voice.

Then the Three Bears went
upstairs into their bedroom.
Now the girl had moved
the pillow on the Great,
Huge Bear's bed.

"Someone's been sleeping in my bed!"

said the Great, Huge Bear, in his great, rough, gruff voice.

And the girl had moved the bolster on the Middle Bear's bed.

"Someone's been sleeping in my bed!" said the Middle Bear, in his middle voice.

And when the Small, Wee Bear
came to look at his bed, there upon
the pillow was the girl's head.

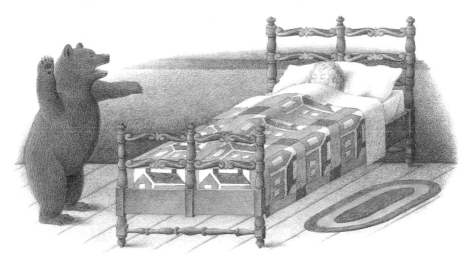

"Someone's been sleeping in my bed, and there she is!"

said the Small, Wee Bear,

in his small, wee voice.

When the girl heard the small, wee voice of the Small, Wee Bear, it woke her at once. Up she started, and when she saw the Three Bears on one side of the bed, she tumbled herself out the other and ran to the window. Out the girl jumped, and she ran away home.

The Three Bears never saw anything more of her. They cleaned up their house, and then they lived happily ever after.

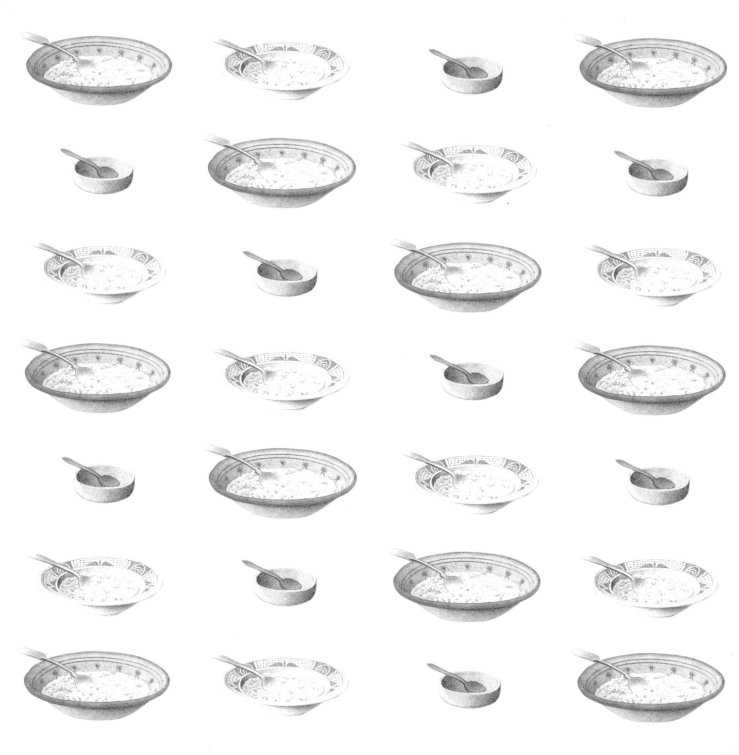